# POKéMON ®

## WELCOME TO SINNOH

## ACTIVITY BOOK

Written by
Sonia Sander

Cover & Interior designed by Kay Petronio

ISBN-13: 978-0-545-11383-0
ISBN-10: 0-545-11383-0

12 11 10 9 8 7 6 5 4 3 2 1                    8 9 10 11 12/0

Printed in the U.S.A.
First printing, November 2008

SCHOLASTIC INC.
New York   Toronto   London   Auckland   Sydney
Mexico City   New Delhi   Hong Kong   Buenos Aires

# A-MAZE-ING SINNOH

Ash just arrived in Sinnoh. Help him find his friend Brock!

ASH

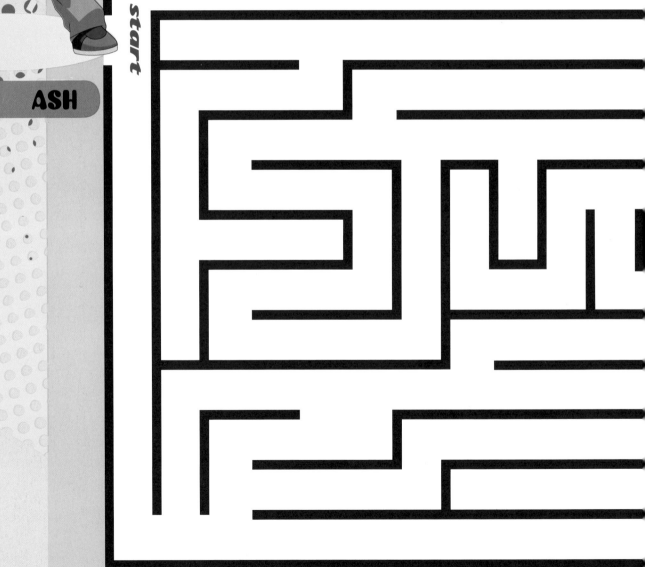

start

Ash takes a ferry to get to Sinnoh.

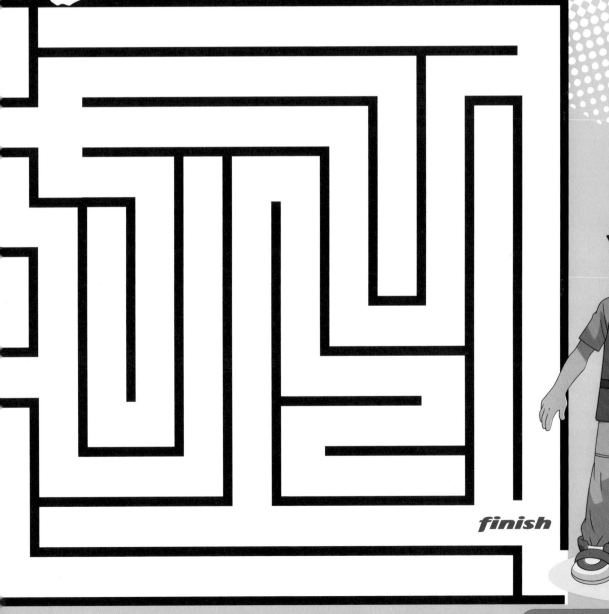

finish

BROCK

# NAME THAT POKÉMON

Can you tell who's who?
Under each close-up, fill in
the name of the Pokémon
famous for that detail.

Mime Jr. likes
places where
people gather.

**1** _____

**2** _____

**3** _____

**4** _____

**5** _____

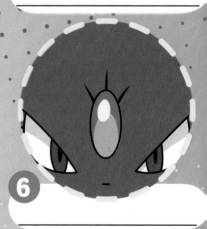

**6** _____

**7** _____

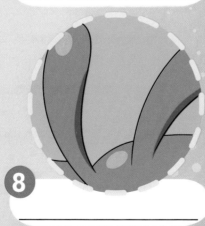

**8** _____

**9** _____

 Bonsly    Buizel    Mime Jr.    Weavile    Mantyke    Chatot    Turtwig    Chimchar    Piplup

# POKÉMON EVOLUTION

How well do you know how your Pokémon evolve? Match the first column to their correct evolutions.

Mime Jr.

Kricketune

Bonsly

Bibarel

Bidoof

Mr. Mime

Kricketot

Sudowoodo

# FRIEND SEARCH

Circle the names of Ash and his friends hidden in the puzzle below. Look up, down, forward, backward, and diagonally.

*ASH*
*BROCK*
*DAWN*
*PIKACHU*
*TURTWIG*
*CHIMCHAR*
*PIPLUP*

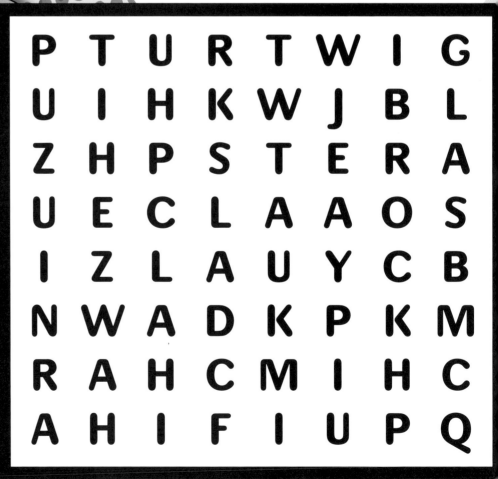

```
P T U R T W I G
U I H K W J B L
Z H P S T E R A
U E C L A A O S
I Z L A U Y C B
N W A D K P K M
R A H C M I H C
A H I F I U P Q
```

# POKÉMON MATCH UP

Can you tell which shadow belongs to which Pokémon?

Diagla is able to control and alter time.

Palkia is able to warp space.

# WATER, WATER EVERYWHERE!

Lots of Water-type Pokémon live in the Sinnoh Region. But one of the characters below is not one of them! Can you tell which Pokémon does not belong with the others?

Pachirisu is an Electric-type Pokémon.

# POKÉMON MESSAGE

Use the clues below to decode the hidden Pokémon message.

A =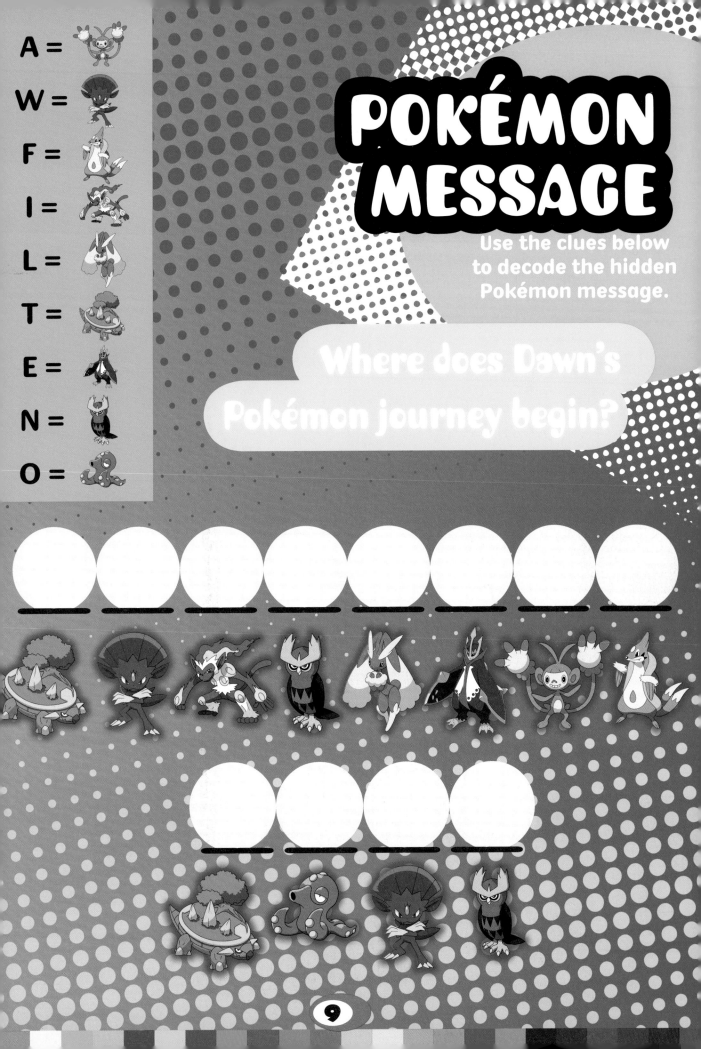
W =
F =
I =
L =
T =
E =
N =
O =

Where does Dawn's Pokémon journey begin?

9

# PEEK-A-BOO, IT'S...

Connect the dots to reveal this Pokémon favorite.

This Pokémon's evolved form is Raichu.

Who is it? Write your answer on the line below.

# POKÉMON BATTLE

This Pokémon loves honey! Sometimes it even steals it from Combee.

Ash is ready for anything. But who's waiting for him in the Eterna Forest? Connect the dots to reveal the hidden Pokémon.

Who is it? Write your answer on the line below.

# COLOR KEY

If Cherrim is blooming, the sun must be shining! Color by number to make Cherrim bright and happy!

1

1

1

1

3

1

3

1

1

2

1

1

3

1

4

1

1

2

2

Cherrim turns back into a bud whenever the sunlight dwindles.

12

# TYPE TWIST

The Bug-type Pokémon have been confused with the Normal-types! Can you tell them apart? Circle the Bug-types to fix the mix-up!

# HOW TO DRAW

You can draw Cranidos and Shieldon, too. Just work on one square at a time.

Cranidos and Shieldon both lived in jungles 100 million years ago!

# POKÉMON EVOLUTION

Starly was the first Pokémon Ash caught in Sinnoh.

You've already matched Pokémon through one evolution. Can you match these Pokémon through two? Start with the first column, and draw an arrow to its evolved form. Then go one step farther, to column three.

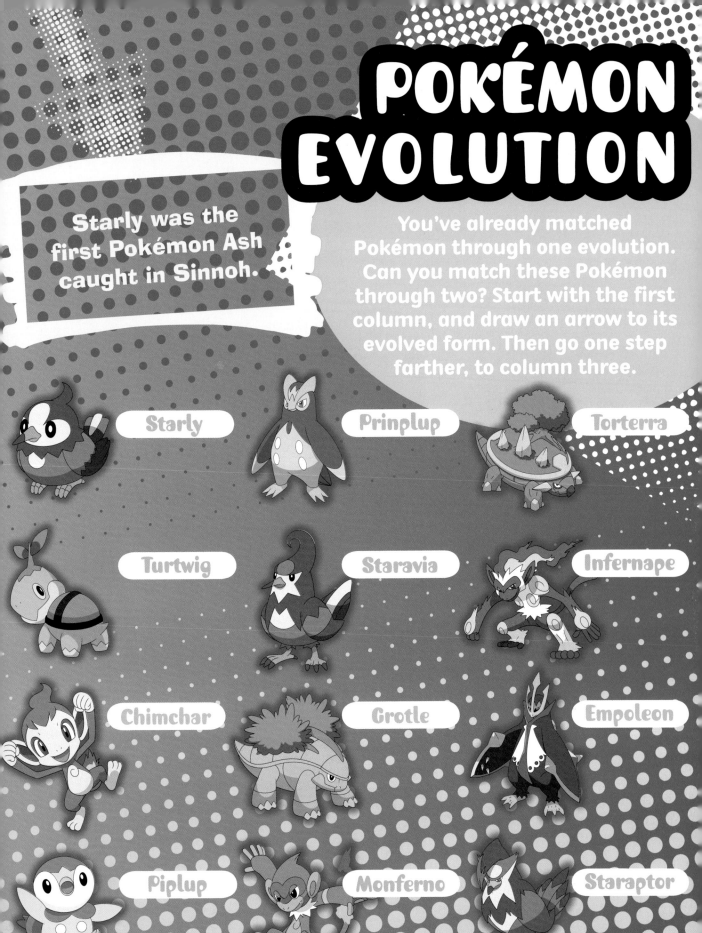

Starly

Prinplup

Torterra

Turtwig

Staravia

Infernape

Chimchar

Grotle

Empoleon

Piplup

Monferno

Staraptor

# NAME THAT POKÉMON

Can you tell who's who a second time? Under each close-up snapshot, fill in the name of the Pokémon famous for that detail.

**1** _____

**2** _____

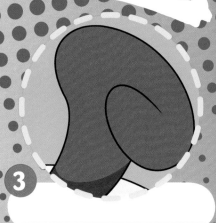

**3** _____

**4** _____

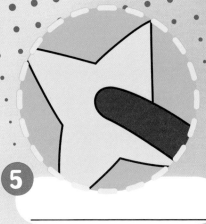

**5** _____

**6** _____

**7** _____

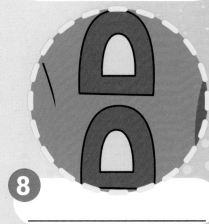

**8** _____

**9** _____

 **Bastiodon**   **Buneary**   **Shinx**   **Pachirisu**   **Pikachu**   **Rampardos**   **Kricketot**   **Roserade**   **Starly**

# HIDE-AND-SEEK

Connect the dots to help Dawn and Brock uncover their lost Pokémon.

Who is it? Write your answer on the line below.

2 _____

Who is it? Write your answer on the line below.

1 _____

# POKÉ BALL

Which Pokémon is hidden in each of these Poké Balls? Match each Pokémon to one of the Poké Balls on the right.

So proud it won't even accept food from Trainers.

Type: Water

Height: 1' 04"

Weight: 11.5 lbs

Likes to climb rocky cliffs.

Type: Fire

Height: 1' 08"

Weight: 13.7 lbs

Has an earthen shell that hardens when it drinks water.

Type: Grass

Height: 1' 04"

Weight: 22.5 lbs

# POKÉMON CODE

Use the clues below to reveal the secret question. Do you know the answer? Write it on the dotted line.

## W H I C H

## POKÉMON

## U S E S A

## S E C R E T

## C O D E ?

## W E A V I L E

---

S =

E =

A =

H =

W =

U =

I =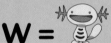

R = 

D = 

T = 

O = 

C =

# COPYCAT!

Can you guess who is able to mimic its foes' movements? Connect the dots to check your answer.

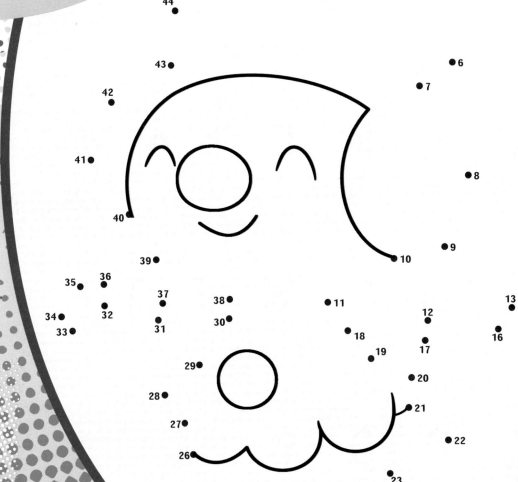

Who is it? Write your answer on the line below.

Mime Jr. loves mimicking people and Pokémon.

# TRAINER TANGLE

Follow the lines to find out which Pokémon belongs with each Trainer.

START

FINISH

# TEAM ROCKET ESCAPE

Team Rocket is after Pikachu! Can Ash and his friends make their way safely through the forest without bumping into them?

# ANSWER KEY

## P 2-3
start ... finish

## P 4
1. Turtwig
2. Piplup
3. Chimchar
4. Bonsly
5. Mime Jr.
6. Weavile
7. Chatot
8. Mantyke
9. Buizel

## P 5
Mime Jr.
Kricketune
Bonsly
Bibarel
Bidoof
Mr. Mime
Kricketot
Sudowoodo

## P 6
```
P T U R T W I G
U I H K W J B L
Z H P S T E R A
U E C L A O C S
I Z L A U Y C B
N W A D K P K M
R A H C M I H C
A H I F I U P Q
```

## P 7

## P 8

## P 9
Answer: Twinleaf Town

## P 10
Pikachu

## P 11
Mothim

## P 13

## P 15
Starly · Prinplup · Torterra
Turtwig · Staravia · Infernape
Chimchar · Grotle · Empoleon
Piplup · Staraptor
Monferno

## P 16
1. Starly
2. Roserade
3. Kricketot
4. Pachirisu
5. Shinx
6. Rampardos
7. Buneary
8. Bastiodon
9. Pikachu

## P 17
1 Pachirisu
2 Croagunk

## P 18

## P 19
**Hidden Question:**
Which Pokémon uses a secret code?
**Answer: Weavile**

## P 20
Mime Jr.

## P 21

## P 22-23
start ... finish